The Little Prince

ANTOINE DE SAINT-EXUPÉRY

Antoine de Saint-Exupéry, born Antoine Marie Jean-Baptiste Roger (1900-1944), was a French writer, poet, and pioneering aviator. He became a laureate of several of France's highest literary awards and also won the U.S. National Book Award. He is best remembered for his novella *The Little Prince (Le Petit Prince)* and for his lyrical aviation writings, including *Wind, Sand and Stars* and *Night Flight*.

JUOK YOON

Ju Ok Yoon holds a Ph.D. in Medieval Studies in English Literature from the University of Massachusetts-Amherst with concentrations in Anglo-Norman and Middle English romances. She is an HK research professor at the Institute of the Humanities at Yonsei University, Seoul, Korea. In addition to romances, she has interests in literate culture, epistolarity, poetic iconicity, woundology, and food as research topics. One of her recent translations includes *Rethinking Writing* by Roy Harris, which was recognized as a distinguished scholarly work by the Korean Ministry of Culture (Se-Jong-Do-Seo) in 2014. Currently, she is working on the reinterpretation of medieval and early modern English literature for young Korean readers.

MINJI KIM

Minji Kim has been illustrating online games developed by JC Entertainment. She also designed and color coordinated the characters for the animation movie, Ark. Ms. Kim's illustration works include *The Little Prince*, *The Prince and the Pauper*, *The Wizard of OZ*, *Peter Pan*, and many others.

SARA TOTTEN

Sara Totten is a writer and editor residing in Western Massachusetts, U.S.A. She holds a Master of Arts in English Rhetoric and Composition from Arizona State University.

| TRANSLATOR'S NOTE |

More than anything, it is a pure joy and a tremendous privilege that I was given a rare opportunity to translate this beautiful world classic *The Little Prince* (Le Petit Prince) from French into English. As a translator, I have mixed feelings now. I feel relieved naturally because the work is through at last. Strangely, however, I also have a sense of sadness, perhaps because I can no longer keep the little prince only to myself and instead have to let go of him, just as the "I" in the story has to do. It was a long time ago, nearly three decades ago or even earlier, that I first read this contemplative French novella in Korean translation, never dreaming then that I would be translating it into English in my mid-forties.

When my Korean publisher first offered me this translation project, I could not be assured of its success for multiple reasons, one of which is perhaps explained by the anxiety that I might not be able to accomplish it to the level of perfection I desired. But I am proud that I overcame that fear and decided to carry it out. Surely, it must have been quite an adventure on the publisher's side, too, to decide to issue a new English translation of this French story into the market in which dozens of English translations already exist worldwide. Hence, I wholeheartedly wish that the publisher's unstinting commitment to this project will prove to be rewarding in all respects.

I would like readers to know that as reader and interpreter I have paid my utmost affection and tribute to the original text by remaining faithful to it to the very best of my abilities. But I also want readers to understand the reality that translation in essence involves interpretations, meaning that more often than not I was obliged to crack open and create valid meanings out of the words, phrases, or sentences that seemed to resist my efforts to obtain access to their innermost roots. Indeed, my sensitivity and training as a student of English literature, as well as my long-sustained fondness for *The Little Prince*, helped me immensely to make my paths out of such maze-like moments.

I should also add that numerous long-distance communications with my American editor, Ms. Sara Totten, played an indispensable part in sculpting the best meanings and expressions in English. I am thrilled to present this new English translation of *Le Petit Prince* not only to Korean readers who will be its main audience, as I know, but also to any readers around the world who understand English and crave heart-touching literature. I have full confidence that the dream-like illustrations of Ms. Min Ji Kim will perfect the beauty of the text and impress many new and veteran fans of the little prince, who might be small but whose mind is great and full of compassion and clairvoyance.

Ju Ok Yoon

| 역자서문 |

　　전 세계인들로부터 많은 사랑을 받아온 명작 고전인 생 텍쥐페리의 『어린왕자』(Le Petit Prince)를 한국에서는 처음으로 원어인 불어에서 영어로 번역하는 작업을 할 수 있었다는 것은 저에게는 큰 기쁨이자 영광이었습니다. 번역을 완료한 이 시점에 역자로서 남다른 감회를 느낍니다. 번역을 잘 마무리했다는 점에서 안도감을 느끼지만 동시에 지난 몇 달 동안 가슴속에 소중하게 품어왔던 어린왕자를 이제는 놓아주어야 한다는 사실에 마음 한구석이 허전하고 시립니다. 마치 작품 속 화자인 "나"처럼 말입니다. 제가 『어린왕자』를 우리말로 처음 접한 때는 삼십여 년 전으로 기억합니다. 그때는 제가 어른이 되어서 이 훌륭한 고전 작품을 영어로 번역하리하고는 상상도 못했습니다.

　　인디고 출판사로부터 『어린왕자』 불영 번역 제안을 받았을 때 처음에는 여러 가지 이유로 많이 망설였습니다. 망설인 이유 중 하나는 아마도 제가 원하는 수준만큼 이 아름다운 작품을 완벽하게 번역해 내지 못할 수도 있다는 부담감이었을 것입니다. 그런 부담감에도 불구하고 용기를 낸 것은 참 잘한 일인 것 같습니다. 생각해 보면 전 세계적으로 수십 개의 『어린왕자』 영어 번역이 이미 존재하는 상황에서 새로운 불영 번역을 시도한 점은 출판사의 입장에서도 큰 모험이었을 것입니다. 그렇기 때문에 더욱더 역자로서 이 책이 많은 독자들로부터 사랑을 받았으면 하는 바람입니다.

    이 작품을 아끼는 독자 중 한 사람이자 역자로서 저의 능력이 허락하는 한 최대한 원작에 충실하려 했습니다. 동시에 번역이라는 작업이 어쩔 수 없이 새로운 해석의 과정이라는 점 또한 독자들께서 이해해주셨으면 합니다. 종종 가장 내밀한 속살을 드러내기를 거부하는 듯한 단어, 구, 문장들을 열어서 거기로부터 의미를 만들어 내는 과정은 마치 미로를 헤매는 듯한 아득한 경험이었으며, 그때마다 『어린왕자』에 대한 저의 오래된 애정과 더불어, 문학에 대한 저의 감수성, 그리고 영문학자로서 제가 받은 오랜 훈련이 많은 도움이 되었습니다.

    특히, 영어로 최상의 의미와 표현을 조각해내는 데에는 미국 뉴잉글랜드에 거주하는 원어민 편집자 Sara Totten과 이메일로 나누었던 수많은 토론이 필수적이었음을 밝혀두고 싶습니다. 한국 독자들뿐 아니라 마음을 따뜻하게 해줄 문학 작품을 영어로 읽기를 원하는 세계의 모든 독자들에게 이『어린왕자』영어 번역을 자신 있게 권합니다. 김민지 일러스트 작가의 삽화들이 텍스트의 아름다움을 배가시켜 줄 것이라 확신합니다.『어린왕자』를 처음 읽는 독자들뿐만 아니라 오래전부터 이 작품을 사랑해온 독자들도 작은 몸집에 큰 마음과, 삶과 세상에 대한 연민과 예지력으로 충만한 어린왕자를 더욱 더 사랑해주시기를 바랍니다.

2015년 봄에
역자 윤주옥

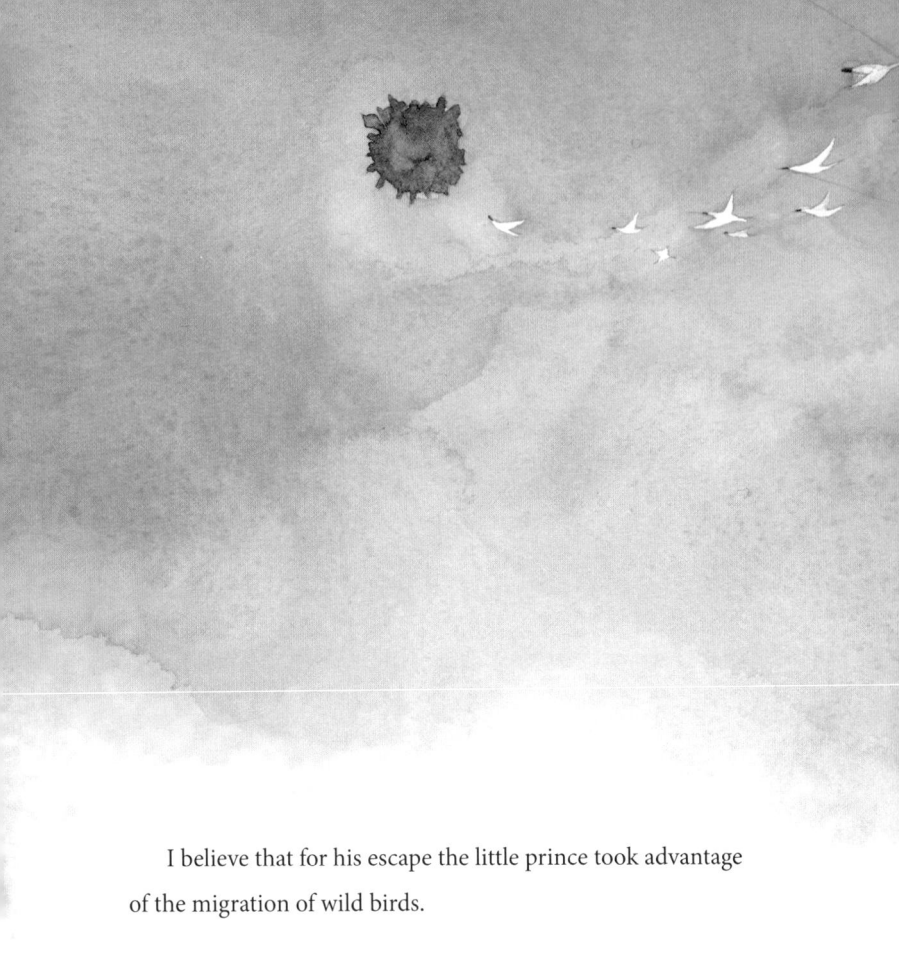

I believe that for his escape the little prince took advantage of the migration of wild birds.

TO LÉON WERTH

I ask children to pardon me
for dedicating this book to a grown-up.
I have a serious excuse: This grown-up is the very best friend
that I have in the world.
I have another excuse: This grown-up can understand
everything, even children's books.
I have a third excuse: This grown-up lives in France,
where he is hungry and cold. He needs much consolation.
If all of these excuses are not sufficient,
I would like to dedicate this book to the child
who my grown-up friend once was in the past.
All grown-ups used to be children once.
(However, very few of them remember it!)
Therefore, I correct my dedication as such:

To LÉON WERTH
when he was a little boy

01

When I was six year old, I saw a magnificent image in a book called *True Stories*, a book about the virgin forest. It depicted a boa constrictor that was devouring a wild animal whole. Here is a copy of the picture:

It said in the book: "Boa constrictors swallow their prey, bones and all, without chewing it. Afterward, they cannot move, so they sleep for six whole months while they digest."

Then I pondered a great deal over adventures in the jungle. After some practice with a colored pencil, I succeeded in drawing my first picture. My Picture Number 1. It looked like this:

I showed my masterpiece to the grown-ups, and then I asked them if my picture frightened them. They answered me: "Why on earth would a hat be frightening?"

My picture did not represent a hat. It showed a boa constrictor that had swallowed an elephant. After that, I drew the inside of the snake, in order that the grown-ups could understand it. They always have to have things explained to them. This is my Picture Number 2:

Then, the grown-ups advised me to put aside my pictures of boa constrictors, either their insides or their outsides, and instead to be interested in geography, history, mathematics, and grammar. This is how I, at the age of six, gave up the wonderful career of drawing. I was discouraged from the failures of my Picture Number 1 and Picture Number 2.

Grown-ups never understand anything on their own, and it is tiresome for children to have to explain things to them all the time.

Therefore, I had to choose a different job, and I learned how to pilot airplanes. I have flown everywhere in the world. And, indeed, geography has helped me a great deal. I can tell, at first sight, China from Arizona. Geography is quite useful if you get lost during the night.

In this way, I have had much contact with many serious people in the course of my life. I have had much experience with grown-ups. I have watched them very closely. But it has not much improved my opinion of them.

Whenever I encountered grown-ups who seemed brilliant to me, I did the experiment of making them take a look at my Picture Number 1 which I always carried with me. I wanted to know if they truly understood it. But they answered me back: "It's a hat." So, I never told them about boa constrictors, or virgin forests, or stars. I stooped to their level. I talked to them about bridge, golf, politics, and ties. And they became very pleased to know such a sensible man.

02

So, I lived alone, without anyone to really talk with, until my airplane broke down in the Sahara Desert six years ago. Something inside the engine was broken. Since I had no mechanic or passenger with me, I readied myself to try to carry out the difficult repair work all by myself. For me, it was a matter of life and death. I scarcely had enough water to drink for a week. On the first night, I slept on the sand, a thousand miles away from a place where anyone lived. I was more isolated than the survivor of a shipwreck on a raft drifting in

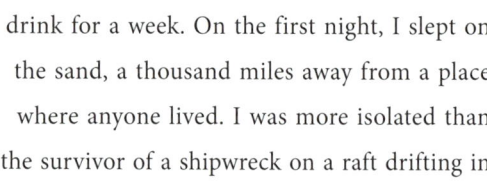

the middle of the ocean.

Thus, you can imagine how very surprised I was when, at the break of day, an odd and small voice woke me.

The voice said: "Please… draw me a sheep."

"Pardon me?"

"Draw me a sheep."

I jumped to my feet, as if I had been struck by lightning. I rubbed my eyes hard. I looked about intently. Then I saw a small but absolutely extraordinary boy who looked at me very seriously. This is the best portrait of him that I, much later, succeeded in drawing.

However, my picture is certainly much less delightful than the actual model. It is not my fault. I was discouraged by grown-ups from taking on the career of drawing at the age of six, and I learned nothing about drawing, except for the insides and outsides of boa constrictors.

So, I was surprised, and I stared at the fellow with wide eyes. Don't forget that I was a thousand miles away from where anyone lived. But it did not seem to me that the little boy was

either lost or dying of fatigue, hunger, thirst, or fear. He never looked like a child who had strayed into the middle of the desert, a thousand miles away from any villages.

When I was finally able to speak, I asked him:

"But…what on earth are you doing here?"

Then, he said to me, very gently, as if he were asking a very serious thing:

"Please…draw me a sheep."

When a mystery is too powerful, we do not dare to disobey it. However absurd it seemed to me, far, far away from any villages, and even in danger of death, I took out a sheet of paper and a fountain pen from my pocket. Then, I remembered how I had come to study geography, history, mathematics, and grammar, and I told the little fellow in a slightly irritated tone that I did not know how to draw.

He replied to me:

"It does not matter. Draw me a sheep..."

Now since I had never drawn a sheep, I drew once again one of the only two pictures that I was capable of drawing: The picture of the boa constrictor from the outside. And I was stunned when the little boy responded:

"No! No! I do not want an elephant inside of a boa constrictor. A snake is too dangerous, and an elephant is too cumbersome. On my planet, everything is very small. I need a sheep. Draw me a sheep."

Then, I drew again.

He watched attentively, and then he said:

"No! That sheep is already too sickly. Draw me another sheep."

I made another drawing.

My friend smiled kindly and indulgently:

"As you yourself can well see, this is not sheep, it is a ram. It has horns."

So I drew a picture again.

But he refused it, just like the previous pictures.

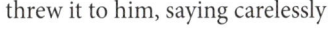

"It is too old. I want a sheep that will live for a long time."

Then, running out of patience, because I was in a hurry to start taking apart the engine, I hastily scrawled a drawing and I threw it to him, saying carelessly:

"It is a box. The sheep that you want is inside."

I was much surprised to see that the face of my young judge brightened:

"It is absolutely how I would like to see the sheep. Do you think that he needs much grass?"

"Why?"

"Because on my planet everything is quite small."

"It will certainly be fine. I drew you a very small sheep."

He bent his head over the picture:

"He is not that small. Look! He has gone to sleep."

And this is the way that I became acquainted with the little prince.

03

It took me a long time to understand where he came from. The little prince, who threw so many questions at me, never seemed to listen to my questions. From words that were dropped by chance, everything was revealed to me little by little. When he noticed my airplane for the first time (I will not draw my airplane, because it is too complicated for me to do so), he asked me:

"What is this thing?"

"It is not a mere thing. It flies. It is an airplane. It is my airplane."

And I was proud to let him know that I had flown. Then, he

exclaimed:

"What! You fell from the sky!"

"Yes," I said modestly.

"Oh! That is funny."

Then, the little prince roared with laughter, which irritated me quite a bit. I want people to take my misfortunes seriously.

Then, he added:

"Then, you also fell from the sky! What planet are you from?"

I immediately glimpsed a light into the mystery of his appearance, and I abruptly questioned him:

"Did you come from another planet?"

However, he made no answer to me. He nodded his head gently, still looking at my airplane:

"It is true that you cannot have come from far away."

And he sank into a reverie that lasted a long while. Then, taking the picture of his sheep out of his pocket, he buried his head in contemplating his treasure.

You can imagine how very intrigued I was by this half-confessed secret about the "other planets". So I strived to find out more about this:

"My little friend, where are you from? Where is 'my planet'? Where do you want to take your sheep picture?"

He said to me after a meditative silence:

"It is good that the box that you have given me will serve as a house for the sheep at night."

"Certainly. And if you are nice, I will also draw you a rope to tie the sheep with during the day. And a post."

This new offer seemed to shock the little prince:

"To tie him? What an odd idea that is!"

"But if you do not tie him, the sheep will wander everywhere, and he will get lost."

My friend gave another burst of laughter:

"But where would he go?"

"Anywhere. Wherever his eyes might lead."

Then, the little prince solemnly remarked:

"It does not matter, because on my planet everything is so small!"

And, with perhaps a hint of sadness, he added:

"Straight in front of him, he cannot go very far."

04

This is how I learned the second important thing. The planet that he came from was hardly bigger than a house! It did not surprise me much, though. I well knew that, aside from large planets like Earth, Jupiter, Mars, and Venus, which people have named, there are hundreds of other planets, some of which are so small that it is difficult to see them even with a telescope. When an astronomer discovers one of these planets, he gives it a number for a name. For example, he might call it "Asteroid 325".

I have serious reason to believe that the planet that the little prince came from is Asteroid B612. This asteroid has been seen only once before with a telescope, in 1909, by a Turkish astronomer.

The astronomer then gave a grand presentation at the International Congress of Astronomy about what he had discovered. But nobody would believe him because of his Turkish costume. Grown-ups are like that…

Fortunately for the reputation of Asteroid B612, a Turkish dictator imposed upon his people under pain of death that they dress themselves in European style. The astronomer gave his presentation once again in 1920, in a very elegant outfit. This time the whole world agreed upon his discovery.

If I have told you about the details of Asteroid B612, and if I have told you its number, it is on account of the grown-ups. The grown-ups love numbers. When you tell them about a new friend of yours, they never ask you about the essentials. They never ask you: "What is his voice like? What sorts of games does he like to play? Does he collect butterflies?" Instead, they ask you:

"How old is he? How many brothers does he have? How much does he weigh? How much money does his father make?" Then, based only on these figures, they believe that they know him. If you said to the grown-ups: "I have seen a beautiful house of rosy bricks, with geraniums at the windows and doves on the roof," they would be unable to imagine such a house. Instead, you must tell them: "I have seen a house that is worth one hundred thousand francs." Then they will exclaim, "How wonderful that house is!"

So, if you say to the grown-ups: "The proof that a little prince existed is that he was delightful, that he laughed, and that he wanted a sheep. When a person wants a sheep, that is proof that he exists," they would shrug their shoulders and treat you like a child. If you tell them instead: "The planet that he came from is Asteroid B612," then they will be persuaded, and they will leave you in peace without troubling you with any more questions. Grown-ups are like that. You should not be offended because of it. Children must be very lenient with grown-ups.

But, of course, we who understand life, we do not care much about numbers. I would have liked to begin this story in the manner of telling fairy tales: "Once upon a time, there was a little prince who lived on a planet that was scarcely bigger than he himself, and who needed a friend…" For those who understand life, this would ring far truer.

I do not want people to read my book thoughtlessly. I feel very sad, talking about these memories. It has been six years already since my friend went away with the drawing of his sheep. If I try to describe him here, it is because I do not want to forget him. It is sad to forget a friend. Not all people have had a friend. If I forgot him, I would become like the grown-ups who have no interests except numbers. Again, this is why I bought a box of paints and some crayons. It is hard to take up drawing again at my age because I had not attempted to try something different other than to draw the inside and the outside of a boa constrictor since the age of six. Of course, I will try to draw his portraits as like to him as possible. Nonetheless, I cannot be certain that I will be successful. One drawing is done all right, but the other one does not look like him. I make some mistakes about his height, too. First, the little prince looks too tall. Then, he looks too small. I also hesitate about the color of his costume. I fumble along with great difficulty, now trying this and now trying that. Finally, I might make other incorrect choices about important details. Despite all this, I must be pardoned. My friend never explained anything to me. Perhaps he believed that I was like

him. Unfortunately, however, I do not know how to see sheep through the walls of boxes. Perhaps I am a little bit like the grown-ups. I have had to grow old.

05

Every day, I learned something about his planet, about his departure, and about his voyage. It came about very slowly, by chance. This is the way that I, on the third day, came to know about the tragedy of the baobab trees.

This time, it was again thanks to the sheep, for the little prince all of a sudden asked me, as if filled with great doubt:

"It is quite true that sheep eat bushes, isn't it?"

"Yes. It is true."

"Oh! I am pleased."

I did not understand why it was so important whether or not

sheep eat bushes. Then, the little prince continued:

"Therefore, they also eat baobab trees, don't they?"

I pointed out to the little prince that, first, baobab trees were not bushes but big trees, as tall as churches, and also that, even if he brought in a whole herd of elephants, they would not eat their way through even one baobab tree.

The idea of a herd of elephants made the little prince laugh:

"You would have to stack up elephants upon elephants."

Then, he pointed out wisely:

"Before they grow tall, baobab trees first start small."

"Indeed! But why do you want your sheep to eat the little baobab trees?"

He said, "Well! You know!" as if he were talking about something self-evident. And it took great effort for me to figure out the matter on my own.

And, indeed, on the planet of the little prince, just as on all other planets, there were both good and bad plants. Of course, good seeds are from good plants, and bad seeds from bad ones. However, seeds are hidden. They sleep in the secret of the soil until one of them has the whim to wake up. Then, the seed stretches and pushes a small, harmless, and beautiful shoot shyly toward the sun. If it is a shoot of radish or rosebush, you can let it push itself out as it wants. But if it is a bad plant, you have to pull it out right away, as soon as you recognize it. Now, there were terrible seeds on the planet of the little prince. They were the seeds of the baobab trees. The soil of the planet was overrun with them. If you are too late to act, you can never get rid of a baobab tree. It will clutter up the entire planet. It can even puncture holes in the planet with its roots. And if the planet is too small, and if the baobab trees are too many, then they even can make the planet burst apart.

"It is a matter of discipline," the little prince said to me later. "When you finish washing yourself up in the morning, you have to put things in order very carefully on my planet. You regularly have to force yourself to pull out the baobab trees the moment you distinguish them from the rosebushes. When they are very young, the trees look very much like rosebushes. It is very tedious but very easy work to pull out the trees."

And, one day the little prince advised me to draw a fine picture in order to make the lesson clear in the heads of children where I live. He said to me:

"If they travel someday, it will help them. Sometimes, it is not a problem to put off your work. When it comes to the baobab trees, however, it always means a catastrophe. I knew a planet where a lazy fellow lived. He neglected three little bushes…"

Following the instruction of the little prince, I drew a picture of the planet. I hardly like to take the tone of a moralist. However, the danger of the baobab trees is barely known, and the risk to someone who gets lost on an asteroid would be so high that I decided to make an exception this time and to drop my reserve. I said: "Children, watch out for the baobab trees!"

I made many efforts to draw this picture because I wanted to warn my friends of the danger that they, just like myself, have long been unaware of. The lesson that I pass on this way is worth all of the efforts that I made.

Probably, you are wondering: "Why is there no other picture as spectacular as the one of the baobab trees in this book?"

The answer is very simple. I have tried, but the others did not work out so well. When I was drawing the baobab trees, I was driven by a sense of urgency.

06

Oh, little prince, I gradually understood your melancholic little life. For a long time, the only diversion that you had was the delight of the sunset. I learned this new detail on the morning of the fourth day when you told me:

"I am very fond of the sunset. Let's watch the sunset."

"But we have to wait."

"Wait for what?"

"Wait for the sun to go down."

You seemed to be very surprised at first, and then you laughed at yourself. You said to me:

"I always think that I am at home!"

Indeed! Everybody knows that when it is noon in the United States, the sun is going down over France. It would be wonderful to be able to set off to France in a moment and observe the sunset. Unfortunately, France is too far away. However, on your small planet, little prince, you could simply pull your chair over a few steps and watch the twilight whenever you wanted to...

"One day, I watched the sun go down forty-three times!"

And a little later you added:

"You know, when people are really sad, they love to watch the sunset."

"Were you very sad on the day that you watched the sunset forty-three times, then?"

But he made no answer to me.

07

On the fifth day, once again thanks to the sheep, the secret of the life of the little prince was revealed to me. He asked me abruptly, with no forewarning, as if asking about the consequence of a problem that has been meditated in silence for a long time:

"As for a sheep, if it eats bushes, does it eat flowers, too?"

"A sheep eats everything that it comes across."

"Even the flowers that have thorns?"

"Yes, even the flowers that have thorns."

"Then, the thorns…what is the use of them?"

I did not know how to answer. At that moment I was very occupied with trying to unscrew a bolt that was too tight on the engine. I had become quite worried because the breakdown of my airplane began to  look very serious and my water was running out, which made me fearful of the worst case.

"The thorns… what is the use of them?"

The little prince never let go of a question, once he had posed it. I had been so worried over the bolt that I replied without thinking much.

"The thorns, they are useless. Flowers have them for pure spite!"

"Oh!"

However, after a moment of silence, he shot back at me, with a sort of grudge:

"I do not believe you! Flowers are weak. They are artless. They reassure themselves as best they can. They believe that they are terrible with their thorns."

I said nothing. At that moment, I was thinking to myself:

'If this bolt continues to be stubborn, I will smash it with a hammer.'

The little prince interrupted my thoughts once again:

"And you know, you know that flowers…"

"No! No! I know nothing. I answered you with the first thing that came to my mind. I am very busy with something serious."

Dumbfounded, he looked at me:

"Something serious!"

He saw me, first the hammer in my hand, then my greasy, black fingers, bending down over an object that looked quite ugly to him.

"You speak just like the grown-ups!"

He made me a bit ashamed. Then, mercilessly, he added:

"You confuse everything. You mix everything up!"

He became extremely angry. He tossed his curly golden hair windward.

"I know a planet where a Mr. Red lives. He has never smelled a flower. He has never looked at a star. He has never loved a person. He does nothing but addition. All day, he repeats what you have just said: 'I am a serious man! I am a serious man!' And he is all puffed up with pride. But he is not a man, he is just a mushroom!"

"He is what?"

"A mushroom!"

The little prince now turned pale with anger.

"Flowers have made thorns for millions of years. Sheep have nonetheless eaten flowers for millions of years. Then isn't it a serious matter to try to understand why flowers go to so much trouble to make thorns that serve no purpose? Isn't the war between the sheep and the flower important? Isn't it more serious and more important than the addition of the plump Mr. Red? And if I know a special flower that exists nowhere else in the whole world except on my planet, and one little sheep can

annihilate her in a single bite one morning, just like that, even without realizing what he is doing, then isn't it important?"

He fumed and then continued:

"If somebody loves a flower that does not exist on millions and millions of stars but only on one single star, then it will make him happy just to look at the stars." He says to himself: 'My flower exists somewhere…' "But if a sheep eats the flower, to him, it will be as if all the stars have lost their lights at once. And do you still think that it is not important?"

The little prince could not continue anymore. He burst suddenly into sobs. The night had fallen. I dropped my tools. I hardly cared about my hammer, the bolt, thirst, or death. There was a little prince who needed be comforted on a star, on a planet, on my planet, on the Earth. I hugged him in my arms and lulled him. I told him:

"The flower that you love is not in danger…I will draw a muzzle for your sheep…I will draw a suit of armor for your flower… I will…"

I had no idea what to say; I felt so awkward. I did not know how to reach him where I could join him again. The realm of tears, it is such a mystery.

08

Very soon I learned about the flower much better. On the planet of the little prince, there had always been flowers that were very simple, were decorated with only one ring of petals, took up no space, and bothered nobody. They would appear in the midst of weeds one morning and then would wither away by evening. But one day, a flower sprouted from a seed blown in from an unknown place, and the little prince watched very closely over this sprout, which looked different from the other sprouts. It could have been a new kind of baobab tree. But the sprout stopped growing and began to prepare a flower. The little prince, who watched the formation of the large bud, felt that a miraculous apparition would emerge from it. Kept in her green chamber, however, the flower did not cease dressing herself to look beautiful. She carefully chose her colors. She dressed herself slowly, adding one petal at a time. She did not want to pop up all rumpled, as poppies do. She did not want to appear except in the full radiance of her beauty. Oh, yes! She was very coquettish! Hence, her mysterious dressing-up continued day after day. And then at last, one morning just as the sun rose, she revealed herself.

She, who had worked hard with such precision, spoke in a yawn:

"Oh, I am not fully awake. Will you pardon me? My petals are still mussed up."

But the little prince could not hold back his admiration:

"How beautiful you are!"

"Am I not?" the flower answered softly. "I was born at the same moment as the sun…"

The little prince soon understood that she

was not very modest, yet she was nonetheless so charming!

Soon she added:

"I believe that it is time for breakfast. Will you be so kind as to think of me?"

And the little prince, utterly confused, looked for a watering can of fresh water and served the flower. In this manner, she very soon began to torment him with her vanity, which was rather annoying. One day, for example, when talking about her four thorns, she said to the little prince:

"They can come, the tigers, with their claws!"

The little prince objected:

"There are no tigers on my planet. Besides, tigers do not eat grass."

The flower replied softly:

"I am not grass."

"Please pardon me…"

"I am not at all afraid of tigers, but I am terrified of drafts. Don't you have a screen?"

The little prince remarked:

"Terrified of drafts…That's very bad for a plant."

And he thought to himself:

'This flower is so complicated.'

"In the evenings, you shall put me under a glass globe. It is very cold on your planet. It is not set up well. The place where I came from…"

But she interrupted herself. She had come in the form of a seed. She could never have known other worlds. Humiliated by letting herself be caught as she began such a naive untruth, she coughed two or three times, in order to place the blame on the little prince.

"The screen?"

"You were talking to me when I was about to look for it!"

Then, she made herself cough, so as to inflict remorse upon him all the more.

In this way, despite all of his good will which had grown out of love, the little prince soon became suspicious of her. He took seriously the things she said that were not important, and then he felt very miserable.

One day, the little prince confided to me:

"I should not have listened to her. No one should listen to

flowers. We should just look at them and smell them. My flower filled my planet with fragrance, but I did not know how to enjoy it. The story about claws, however it disturbed me, should have softened me toward her…"

He also confided to me:

"I was unable to understand anything back then! I should have judged her based not on her words but on her acts. She filled me with fragrance and lit up my life. I should not have run off… I should have seen the tenderness behind her poor trickery. Flowers are so contradictory! But I was too young to know how to love her…"

09

I believe that for his escape the little prince took advantage of the migration of wild birds. On the morning of his departure, he put his planet in order. He carefully swept the active volcanoes. He had two active volcanoes, so they were very helpful for heating breakfast in the morning. He also had one extinct volcano. But, as he said, "Because no one ever knows!" he also swept the extinct volcano carefully. If they are well swept, volcanoes burn gently and regularly, without eruption. Volcanic eruptions are like sparks in a chimney. Obviously, on our planet, we are too small to sweep volcanoes. That is why they give us so

much trouble.

The little prince also looked around for the last shoots of baobab trees with a certain feeling of sadness. He thought that he would never come back. That morning, all of the familiar things looked extremely precious. And when he watered the flower one last time and prepared to shelter her under the globe, he felt like crying.

He said to the flower:

"Good bye."

But she made no reply. He said one more time:

"Good bye."

The flower coughed. But it was not because she was cold. Finally, she said to him:

"I have been foolish. Please, forgive me. I wish you happiness…"

He was surprised that she was not reproachful. He remained very puzzled, holding the globe in the air. He could not understand her calm tenderness.

The flower continued:

"Truly, I have loved you. But you have never known it, and

it is all my fault. That's not important now anyway. But you have been just as foolish as I have. I wish you all happiness. Don't bother yourself with the globe. I do not want it any more."

"But the wind…"

"I am not all that vulnerable to cold. The cool air of the night will do me good. I am a flower."

"But the animals…"

"I will have to put up with two or three caterpillars if I want to get acquainted with some butterflies. It seems that they are very beautiful. Otherwise, who will visit me? You will be far away. As for the big animals, I am not afraid of them. I have my own claws."

And she naively revealed her four thorns. Then she added:

"Stop procrastinating like that. It is irritating me. You have decided to go away. Now, leave!"

It was because she did not want him to see her crying. She was such a proud flower.

10

Within his neighborhood, there were the asteroids 325, 326, 327, 328, 329, and 330. So the little prince began by visiting them in order to look for something to engage and to educate himself.

The first planet was inhabited by a king. Covered in purple and ermine, the king was seated on a very simple yet majestic throne.

"Oh, here comes a subject!" exclaimed the king, when he saw the little prince.

The little prince wondered to himself:

'How could he recognize me when he has never seen me

before?'

The little prince did not know that, for kings, the world is simple. All people are their subjects.

"Come closer to me so that I may see you better," said the king, who was so proud of being a king to somebody at last.

The little prince tried to find a place to sit down, but the whole planet was covered with the magnificent ermine robe. Therefore, he remained standing, and because he was tired, he yawned.

"It is against etiquette to yawn in the presence of a king," the monarch said to the little prince. "I forbid you to do so."

"I cannot refrain from yawning," the little prince, who was very embarrassed, retorted to the king. "I have had a long voyage, and I have not slept much."

"If so," said the king to the little prince, "I order you to yawn. I have not seen anyone yawning for years. So I am very curious about yawning. Come now! Yawn again. That is an order."

"Your order is intimidating me. I can no longer…" said the little prince, turning completely red.

"Hmm! Hmm!" responded the king. "Then, I order you to

yawn sometimes, and sometimes to…"

The king mumbled a bit and looked irritated.

Because the king indeed cared about his authority being respected, he did not tolerate disobedience. He was an absolute monarch. However, because he was a good person, he gave reasonable orders.

The king would say:

"If I ordered…if I ordered a general to change himself into a sea bird, and if he did not obey my order, then it would not be his fault. It would be my fault."

"May I sit down?" asked the little prince timidly.

"I order you to sit down," the king said to the little prince, as he majestically pulled back a tail of his ermine robe.

But the little prince became puzzled. The planet was tiny. Over what could the king reign?

"Sire," said the little prince to the king, "Will you please excuse me if I ask you a question?"

"I order you to ask me a question," the king hastened to assure him.

"Sire…over what do you reign?"

"Over everything," replied the king very simply.

"Over everything?"

With a solemn gesture, the king pointed out his planet, the other planets, and the stars.

"Over all of those?" asked the little prince.

"Over all of them," answered the king.

This was because he was not only an absolute monarch but also a universal monarch.

"And do those stars obey you?"

"Certainly," said the king. "They obey me right away. I do not tolerate disobedience."

Such authority filled the little prince with awe. Had he possessed such power, he would have been able to watch in a single day not forty-four sunsets, but seventy-two, or even a hundred, or even two hundred, never moving his chair! And because he felt a bit sad at the memory of his tiny planet that he had abandoned, he gathered his courage to ask the king a favor:

"I would like to watch a sunset. Please, grant me a favor…Order the sun to set…"

"If I ordered a general to fly from one flower to another in the same manner as a butterfly does, or to write a tragedy, or to change himself into a sea bird, and if he could not carry out the order, whose fault is it, mine or his?"

"It is your fault," answered the little prince firmly.

"Exactly. You must order a man to do what he can do," said the king. "Authority is first based on reason. If you ordered your people to jump into the sea, then a riot would break out. I have the right to demand obedience because my orders are reasonable."

"Then, what about the sunset?" inquired the little prince who never forgot a question once he had asked it.

"The sunset, you shall have it. I shall order it. But I will wait until the conditions become favorable, according to my knowledge of government."

"When will it be?" asked the little prince.

"Hmm! Hmm!" replied the king to the little prince, as he consulted first with a large calendar. "Hmm! Hmm! It will be about… about…it will be in the evening, about 7:40!

And you will see how well I am obeyed."

The little prince yawned. He missed his own sunset. What was more, he already was rather bored.

"I have nothing more to do here," said the little prince to the king. "I shall set off again!"

"Do not go," cried the king, who was so proud of having a subject. "Don't go; I will make you a minister!"

"A minister of what?"

"Of…of justice!"

"But there is no one here to judge!"

"You never know," answered the king. "I have not made a tour of my kingdom yet. I am very old. I have no space for a carriage, and it makes me exhausted to walk around."

"Oh! But I have already seen it," said the little prince, who leaned over to glance once more at the other side of the planet. There was no one there, either.

"Then, you shall judge yourself," said the king. "It is the most difficult thing. It is much more difficult to judge yourself than to judge others. If you succeed in judging yourself well, then it means that you are a true sage."

"As for me," answered the little prince, "I can judge myself wherever I may be. I do not need to live here."

"Hmm! Hmm!" said the king, "I surely know that somewhere on my planet lives an old rat. I hear him at night. You can judge the old rat. You can sentence him to death from time to time. That way, his life will depend on your judgment. However, you will have to pardon him each time, to save him. There is no rat but he."

"As for me," answered the little prince, "I do not like to sentence a death, and I know for certain that I will leave."

"No!" exclaimed the king.

But the little prince, who had completed his preparations for departure, did not want to sadden the old monarch:

"If Your Majesty desires to be obeyed absolutely, Your Majesty should give me a reasonable order. Your Majesty can order me, for example, to leave within one minute. It seems to me that conditions are favorable…"

Since the king made no answer, the little prince at first hesitated, and then sighing, he took his leave.

"I make you my ambassador," shouted the king hurriedly. He

demonstrated a great air of authority.

The little prince thought to himself as he voyaged that the grown-ups were very strange.

11

A Mr. Conceited lived on the second planet.

"Oh! Oh! An admirer is visiting me!" exclaimed Mr. Conceited to himself, as he saw the little prince from afar. Those who are conceited take all others for their admirers.

"Good morning," said the little prince. "You have a funny hat."

"It is a hat for greeting," answered Mr. Conceited to the little prince. "It is for saluting when people acclaim me. Unfortunately, there has been no one who passed my planet."

"Oh yes?" replied the little prince, though he did not quite understand what the man said.

"Clap your hands, one hand against the other," Mr. Conceited directed the little prince.

The little prince clapped his hands, one hand against the other. Then, Mr. Conceited began to salute modestly, raising his hat.

'It is more fun here than on my visit to the king,' said the little prince to himself. Then, he clapped his hands again, one hand against the other. Mr. Conceited saluted again, lifting his hat.

After five minutes, the little prince grew bored with the monotony of the game:

"In order for your hat to come down," asked the little prince, "what do I have to do?"

But Mr. Conceited did not hear him. Those who are conceited listen only when they are being praised.

"Do you really admire me very much?" Mr. Conceited asked the little prince.

"What does it mean to 'admire'?"

"To 'admire' means that you think of me as the most handsome, the most skillful, the richest, and the most intelligent

man on this planet."

"But you are the only one on your planet!"

"Will you do me a favor? To admire me, even so?"

"I admire you," said the little prince, shrugging his shoulders slightly, wondering to himself what difference it could make.

Then, the little prince took his leave.

He thought to himself, as he traveled, that the grown-ups were certainly very strange.

12

The next planet was inhabited by a drunkard. This visit was very short, but it threw the little prince into a deep melancholy:

"What are you doing here?" the little prince asked the drunkard who was settled in silence before a collection of empty bottles and a collection of full bottles.

"I am drinking," answered the drunkard, in a mournful tone.

"Why are you drinking?" asked the little prince.

"In order to forget," answered the drunkard.

"To forget what?" inquired the little prince, who already took pity on him.

"To forget that I am ashamed," confessed the man, dropping his head.

"Ashamed of what?" asked the little prince, who really wanted to help the drunkard out.

"I am ashamed of drinking!" The drunkard finished his words and locked himself up in complete silence.

Perplexed, the little prince took off.

As he continued his voyage, the little prince said to himself that the grown-ups were definitely very, very strange.

13

The fourth planet was the planet of a businessman. The man was so busy that he did not even raise his head when the little prince arrived.

"Hello," said the little prince to the man. "Your cigarette has gone out."

"Three and two makes five. Five and seven makes twelve. Twelve and three makes fifteen. Hello! Fifteen and seven makes twenty-two. Twenty-two and six makes twenty-eight. No time to light up my cigarette again. Twenty-six and five makes thirty-one. Phew! Altogether it makes five hundred and one million six hundred twenty-two thousand seven hundred thirty-one."

"Five hundred million of what?"

"What? Are you still there? Five hundred and one million of…I have forgotten…I have so much work to do! I am a serious man. I do not amuse myself with anything nonsensical. Two and five makes seven…"

"Five hundred and one million of what?" repeated the little prince, who would never let go of a question, once he had posed it.

The businessman raised his head:

"During the fifty-four years that I have lived on this planet, I have been disturbed no more than three times. The first time was twenty-two years ago when a beetle fell. God only knows where it came from. It made such a dreadful noise, and I made four mistakes in one addition. The second time was eleven years ago when I had a fit of rheumatism. I suffer from lack of exercise. I have no time to stroll. I am a serious man. The third time…Well, this is it! As I was saying, five hundred and one million…"

"Millions of what?"

The businessman understood that he would not be left alone in peace:

"Millions of those little things that people sometimes see in the sky."

"Flies?"

"Not at all; the little things that shine."

"Bees?"

"Not at all. The little golden things that idlers daydream about. But I am a serious man! I have no time to daydream."

"Oh! You mean the stars?"

"Yes! The stars."

"And what do you do with five hundred million stars?"

"It is five hundred and one million six hundred twenty-two thousand seven hundred thirty-one stars. I am serious. I am precise."

"And what do you do with those stars?"

"What do I do with them?"

"Yes!"

"Nothing. I possess them."

"You possess the stars?"

"Yes."

"But I already saw a king who…"

"Kings do not possess. They 'reign over'. It is very different."

"So what is the use of possessing the stars?"

"It makes me rich."

"What is the use of being rich?"

"It enables me to purchase more stars when somebody finds them."

The little prince said to himself: 'This man reasons a bit like the drunkard…'

Nevertheless, the little prince asked more questions:

"How is it possible to possess the stars?"

"You mean, to whom do they belong?" replied the businessman grumpily. "I do not know. To nobody. They become mine because I am the one who first thought of it."

"Is that enough?"

"Of course it is. If you find a diamond that belongs to no

one, it becomes yours. When you find an island that belongs to nobody, then it becomes yours. When you have an idea that no one has thought before, then you have a patent on it; it is yours. And, as for me, I possess the stars because nobody before me has thought to possess them."

"That is true," answered the little prince. "But what do you do with the stars?"

"I manage them. I count them, and I count them again," said the businessman. "It is difficult. But I am a serious man."

The little prince was not yet satisfied.

"Well, if I possessed a scarf, I could put it around my neck and keep it. If I possessed a flower, I could pick it up and keep it. But you cannot pick up your stars!"

"No, but I can put them in the bank."

"What do you mean?"

"What I mean is, I write the number of my stars on a small piece of paper. And I lock it with a key in a drawer."

"Is that all?"

"It should suffice!"

"It is funny," thought the little prince. "It is poetic enough.

But it is not very serious."

Regarding things that are serious, the little prince had ideas that differed from the ideas of the grown-ups.

"Well," the little prince continued, "I possess a flower that I water every day. I possess three volcanoes that I sweep every week. I sweep the extinct volcano, too, because you never know what is going to happen. It is somewhat useful to my volcanoes, and it is somewhat useful to my flower, that I possess them. But you are not useful to the stars..."

The businessman opened his mouth to say something, but he could not find a retort, and the little prince went away.

Along his voyage, the little prince said simply to himself that the grown-ups were certainly and absolutely odd.

14

The fifth planet was a very interesting place. It was the smallest of all the planets. There was just enough room for a street lamp and a lamplighter. The little prince could not find an explanation for what a street lamp and a lamplighter were doing on a planet somewhere in the heavens where there were no houses and no people.

Nevertheless, the little prince said to himself:

'Probably this lamplighter is an absurd man. But he is at least less absurd than the king,

Mr. Conceited, the businessman, and the drunkard. At least his work has meaning. When he lights the lamp, it is as if he brought one more star, or one more flower, to life. When he puts out the lamp, it is like putting a flower or a star to sleep. It is a very nice job. It is definitely useful because it is beautiful.'

When he landed on the planet, the little prince saluted the lamplighter respectfully:

"Good morning. Why have you just put out the lamp?"

"Those are the instructions," answered the lamplighter. "Good morning."

"What are the instructions?"

"To put out the lamp. Good evening." And he lit it again.

"But why have you just lit it again?"

"Those are the instructions," replied the lamplighter.

"I don't understand," said the little prince.

"There is nothing to understand," said the lamplighter. "Instructions are instructions. Good morning." Then he put out the lamp.

He wiped his brow with a red-checked handkerchief:

"I have a terrible job. It was sensible in the past. I put the lamp out in the morning and lit it in the evening. During the daytime, I took a rest, and during the night, I slept…"

"Then have the instructions changed since then?"

"The instructions have never changed," said the lamplighter. "That is the real tragedy. From year to year, this planet has turned faster and faster, but the instructions have never changed."

"Really?" said the little prince.

"Yes. Because the planet completes its turn once every minute, I have not a second to rest. I light and put out the lamp once every minute."

"That's funny! On this planet a day lasts only for one minute."

"It is never funny," said the lamplighter. "One month has already passed while we have been talking together."

"One month?"

"Yes. Thirty minutes. Thirty days! Good evening."

Then, the lamplighter lit the lamp again.

The little prince watched him, and he liked the lamplighter who was so faithful to the instructions. He remembered the sunsets that he had gone to look for in the past by pulling up his chair. He wanted to help his friend:

"You know…I know a way for you to have some rest when you want."

"I always long for that," said the lamplighter.

It is possible that people can be both faithful and indolent at once.

The little prince continued:

"Your planet is so small that you can walk all around it in

three strides. All you have to do is to walk slowly enough to always stay in the sunshine. When you feel inclined to take a rest, you just walk, and then daytime will last as long as you want."

"That would not help me much," said the lamplighter. "What I really love to do in life is to sleep."

"That's unfortunate," answered the little prince.

"That's unfortunate," repeated the lamplighter. "Good morning." And he put out the lamp.

As he continued further on his voyage, the little prince said to himself: 'That man, the lamplighter, would be scorned by all the others, by the king, by Mr. Conceited, by the drunkard, by the businessman. Nevertheless, he is the only one who does not seem ridiculous to me. That is perhaps because he cares about something other than himself.'

The little prince gave a sigh of regret and said to himself once again:

'That man is the only one with whom I would like to make friends. But his planet was much too small. There is no room for two people on it.'

The little prince did not dare to confess to himself that he was sorry to leave the planet that was blessed, above all, with one thousand four hundred and forty sunsets in twenty-four hours!

15

The sixth planet was ten times larger than the last one. An old gentleman who wrote enormous books lived there.

"Look! Here comes an explorer!" exclaimed the gentleman when he saw the little prince coming.

The little prince sat down on a table and panted a bit. He had already travelled quite a lot!

"Where are you from?" asked the gentleman.

"What is that big book?" asked the little prince. "What are you doing here?"

"I am a geographer," answered the old man.

"What is a geographer?"

"A geographer is a scholar who knows where seas, rivers, mountains, and deserts are located."

"That sounds very interesting," said the little prince. "Finally, here is a real trade!" Then he took a glance around the planet of the geographer. He had not seen such a majestic planet before.

"Your planet, it is very beautiful. Are there oceans here?"

"I could never know," replied the geographer.

"Oh!" The little prince was disappointed. "What about mountains?"

"I could never know," answered the man.

"What about towns and rivers and deserts?"

"I could not know that either," said the geographer.

"But you are a geographer!"

"That's correct," replied the old man, "but I am not an explorer. There is no explorer on this planet. The geographer does not go out and count the number of towns, rivers, mountains, seas, oceans, and deserts. The geographer is too important to idle about. He does not leave his study. However, he welcomes explorers to it. He questions them and takes notes of their memories. If one of the explorers has memories that seem interesting to him, then the geographer investigates if the explorer is morally sound."

"Why is that?"

"Because an explorer who told lies would bring catastrophe on the books of the geographer. So would an explorer who drank too much."

"How so?" asked the little prince.

"Because drunkards tend to have double vision. Then the geographer would write down two mountains in a place where there is actually only one mountain."

"I know someone," remarked the little prince, "who would make a bad explorer."

"That is possible. Therefore, only when an explorer seems morally sound will the geographer investigate the man's discovery."

"Does the geographer go and see it?"

"No. That would be very complicated. But the geographer requires that an explorer provide proofs. If it is about the discovery of a big mountain, for example, he asks the explorer to bring back big stones from it."

The geographer suddenly grew excited:

"But you, you have come from far away! You are an explorer! Please, describe your planet to me!"

And the old man, who had opened his register, sharpened his pencil. Geographers take notes of the accounts of explorers in pencil first. They wait until explorers provide evidence, and then they write in ink.

"So?" said the old man.

"Oh! On my planet," started the little prince, "there is nothing very interesting; it's very small. I have three volcanoes. Two of them are active, and the other one is extinct. But one never knows."

"One never knows," repeated the geographer.

"I also have a flower."

"We do not take note of flowers," said the old gentleman.

"Why is that? The flower is the prettiest thing."

"It is because flowers are ephemeral."

"What does 'ephemeral' mean?"

"Geographies," said the gentleman, "are the most serious

of all books. They never go out of fashion. It is quite rare for a mountain to change its location. It is extremely rare for an ocean to run out of water. We write about eternal things."

"But extinct volcanoes can awaken again," the little prince cut in. "What does it mean to be 'ephemeral'?"

"Whether volcanoes are extinct or active, it is the same to us geographers," said the old gentleman. "What matters to us is that it is a mountain. It does not change."

"But what does 'ephemeral' mean," repeated the little prince, who would never let go of a question once he had posed it.

"It means to be in danger of imminent death."

"Is my flower in danger of imminent death?"

"Of course."

'My flower is ephemeral,' the little prince said to himself, 'and she has only four thorns to protect herself from the world. And I have left her all alone on my planet!'

It was his first pang of regret. But then he boosted his spirits once again:

"What planet would you like to suggest I visit?" asked the little prince.

"The Earth," answered the geographer to the little prince. "It has a good reputation…"

And the little prince took off, thinking of his flower.

16

Thus the seventh planet was the Earth.

The Earth is not an ordinary planet! There are one hundred and eleven kings (not forgetting, of course, the African kings), seven thousand geographers, nine hundred thousand businessmen, seven and a half million drunkards, three hundred eleven million conceited men; that is to say, about two billion grown-ups.

In hopes of giving you an idea about the size of the Earth, I want to tell you that before electricity was invented, a veritable army of four hundred sixty-two thousand five hundred and eleven lamplighters had to be maintained, if taken together from all of the six continents.

Seen from a bit of a distance, they indeed would look magnificent. The movements of the lamplighters would be well-organized, like those of the ballet in an opera. First would come the turn of the lamplighters of New Zealand and Australia. Done with lighting their lamps, they would go to sleep. Next, the lamplighters of China and Siberia would enter dancing. Then they, too, would slide away behind the scenes. Then would enter the lamplighters of Russia and of the Indies in their turn. Then, those of Africa and Europe. Then, those of South America. Then, those of North America. They would never make a mistake in their order of appearance onstage. It would be quite a spectacle.

Only the lighter of the single lamp at the North Pole and his colleague of the single lamp at the South Pole would lead a life of idleness and nonchalance. They would work twice a year!

17

When people wish to be witty, they sometimes tell little lies. I was not fully honest when I told you about the lamplighters. I took the risk of giving a false idea about our planet to those who do not know it. Human beings occupy only a small portion of the Earth. If the two billion people who inhabit the Earth were to stand upright in a rather crowded manner, as if for an assembly, they would easily fit into one public square twenty miles long and twenty miles wide. You can pile up the entire human race on the smallest island in the Pacific Ocean.

The grown-ups, of course, would not believe this. They

imagine that they take up a great deal of space. They think they are as important as the baobab trees. You should suggest that the grown-ups do the calculations themselves. They adore numbers, and numbers will please them. But do not waste your time at such tasks. It is useless. You may trust me.

When he arrived on the Earth, the little prince was greatly surprised to see no people. He was already afraid that he might have fallen onto the wrong planet when a coil the color of the moon moved about in the sand.

"Good evening," greeted the little prince politely.

"Good evening," replied the snake.

"On what planet have I fallen?" asked the little prince.

"On the Earth, in Africa," answered the snake.

"Oh! So are there no people living on the Earth?"

"We are in the desert. People do not live in the desert. This planet is huge," said the snake.

The little prince sat down on a rock, raised his eyes towards the sky, and said:

"I wonder whether those stars are set alight so that people may recognize their planet some day…Look at my planet. It is

right there above us. But how remote it is!"

"It is beautiful," said the snake. "What has brought you here?"

"I had problem with a flower," answered the little prince.

"Oh!" said the snake.

Then they fell into silence.

"Where are the people?" the little prince asked again at last. "It is rather lonely in the desert."

"You may feel lonely among people, too," said the snake.

The little prince stared at him for a long time.

Finally, the little prince said to the snake:

"You are a funny animal, as thin as a finger."

"But I am far stronger than the finger of a king," replied the snake.

The little prince smiled:

"You are not very strong. You don't even have any feet. You cannot even travel…"

"I can take you further than a ship does," said the snake. It coiled up around the ankle of the little prince, like a golden bracelet.

"The man whom I touch, I can return him to the dust from

whence he came," continued the snake. "But you are innocent, and you have come from a star."

The little prince said nothing to the snake.

"You fill me with pity. You are so weak, on the Earth made of granite. I can help you some day when you miss your planet so much. I can…"

"Oh! I have understood you very well," said the little prince, "but why do you always speak in riddles?"

"I solve them all," replied the snake.

Then they fell into silence again.

18

The little prince travelled the desert and came across only one flower. A flower with three petals, a flower that was nothing special at all…

"Good morning," said the little prince.

"Good morning," replied the flower.

"Where are the people?" asked the little prince courteously. The flower had once seen a caravan passing:

"People? I believe there exist six or seven of them. I saw them years ago. But I have no idea where to find them. They follow the wind. They have no roots, and it gives them a great deal of trouble."

"Good bye," said the little prince to the flower.

"Good bye," replied the flower.

19

The little prince climbed up a high mountain. The only mountains that he had ever known were the three volcanoes that came up to his knees. And he used the extinct volcano as a stool. 'On a mountain as high as this,' the little prince said to himself, 'I will be able to see in one glance all of the planet and all of the people.' However, all he could see were the peaks of very sharp rocks.

"Hello," said the little prince courteously.

"Hello…Hello…Hello," replied the echo.

"Who are you?" asked the little prince.

"Who are you…? Who are you…? Who are you…?" answered the echo.

"Please be my friend, I am all by myself," said the little prince.

"I am all by myself…I am all by myself…I am all by myself," repeated the echo.

The little prince thought to himself: 'How funny this planet is! It is all dry, and all pointed, and all daunting. And the people have no imagination. They repeat what others say to them. On my planet, I had a flower, and she was always the one who spoke first.'

20

However, it happened that the little prince, having walked for a long time through sand, rocks, and snow, finally discovered a road. All roads lead to where people live.

"Good morning," said the little prince. There was a garden where roses were blooming.

"Good morning," replied the roses.

The little prince looked at them. They all resembled his flower.

Greatly confused, he asked them:

"Who are you?"

"We are roses," the flowers replied.

"Oh!" said the little prince.

And he was overcome with great sorrow. His flower had told him that she was the only one of her species in the whole universe. But here were five thousand roses that looked exactly like her, in a single garden!

The little prince said to himself: 'She would be very upset if she saw this. She would cough badly and would pretend to die in order to escape humiliation. Then I should be very much obliged to act as if I were attending to her, because, otherwise, she would let herself really die, in order to humiliate me, too.'

Then he went on: 'I used to believe that I was rich, with one special flower, but all I had was one ordinary flower. One ordinary flower and three volcanoes that came up to my knees, one of which may be extinct forever; they do not make me a great prince at all.'

Lying down in the grass, the little prince began to cry.

21

It was at that moment that the fox appeared.

"Good morning," said the fox.

"Good morning," replied the little prince politely, although as he turned around he saw nothing.

"I am here under the apple tree," said the voice.

"Who are you?" asked the little prince. "You look very pretty."

"I am a fox," answered the fox.

"Come and play with me," the little prince suggested to him. "I am so sad."

The fox said:

"I am not able to play with you. I am not tamed."

"Oh! I am sorry," said the little prince.

But, after thinking, the little prince resumed:

"What does it mean to 'tame'?"

"You are not from here, are you?" asked the fox. "What are you looking for?"

"I am looking for people," answered the little prince. "What does it mean to 'tame'?"

The fox said:

"People, they have guns and they hunt. It is a real problem! They also raise fowl. Those are their only interests. Are you looking for fowl?"

"No," said the little prince. "I am looking for friends. What does it mean to 'tame'?"

"It is an idea that is easily forgotten," answered the fox. "It means to 'create ties'."

"To create ties?"

"Indeed," answered the fox. "To me, you are as yet only one little boy who simply looks like one hundred thousand other little boys. And I have no need of you. And you have no need of me, either. To you, I am nothing more than one fox that just looks like one hundred thousand other foxes. But if you tame me, then we shall need each other. To me, you will be exceptional in the whole wide world. To you, I will be exceptional in the whole wide world."

"I am beginning to understand," said the little prince. "There

is a flower…I believe that she has tamed me…"

"It is possible," said the fox. "On the Earth, there are all sorts of things."

"Oh! She is not on the Earth," said the little prince.

The fox seemed very intrigued:

"You mean, on a different planet?"

"Yes."

"Are there any hunters on the planet?"

"No."

"That is very interesting! What about fowl?"

"No."

"Nothing is perfect," sighed the fox.

However, the fox soon came back around to himself:

"My life is monotonous. I hunt fowl, and people hunt me. All of the fowl look the same, and all of the people look the same. Therefore, I have grown a bit bored. However, if you tame me, then it will be as if my life were lit up by the sun. I will recognize the sound of footsteps that will be different from the sounds of all other footsteps. Other sounds may send me back underground. But your sound will call me out of my hole, like music. And look!

You see, there, the fields of wheat. I do not eat bread. Wheat is of no use to me. The fields of wheat remind me of nothing. And that is a pity. But you have hair of a golden color. So it will be wonderful when you have tamed me! The wheat, which is golden, will remind me of you. And I will love the sound of the wind in the wheat field."

Then, the fox fell silent and looked at the little prince for a long while:

"Will you please tame me?" pleaded the fox.

"I wish I could," replied the little prince, "but I do not have much time. I have friends to discover and many things to know."

"People do not know things unless they tame them," said the fox. "People no longer have time to know anything. They purchase things all ready-made at stores. But stores do not sell friends, so people have no more friends. If you want a friend, then tame me!"

"What do I have to do to tame you?" asked the little prince.

The fox answered:

"You must be very patient. You will first be sitting down, a little remotely from me, like that, in the grass. I shall look at you out of the corners of my eyes, and you will say nothing. Language is the source of misunderstanding. But, each day, you will be sitting a bit closer to me."

The next day the little prince came back.

The fox said:

"It would have been much better if you had come back at the same hour. If you come, for example, at four o'clock in the afternoon, I will begin to feel happy at three o'clock. As the time advances, I shall feel happier and happier. At three o'clock, I will already fidget and grow anxious. I will be able to show you my utter and complete happiness! However, if each time you come at a different hour, then I shall have no idea what time I should get myself ready for you. There should be rituals."

"What is a 'ritual'?" inquired the little prince.

"It is another thing that is easily forgotten," replied the fox. "It makes one day differ from other days, one hour from other hours. For example, hunters have their ritual. Every Thursday, they go and dance with the village girls. This is why Thursdays are wonderful to me. I can go for a long walk, as far as to the vineyard. If the hunters danced anytime, however, then all days would be the same, and I should have no vacation."

In this way, the little prince tamed the fox. Then, as the time of his departure approached:

"Oh!" said the fox, "I feel like crying."

"It is all your fault," said the little prince. "I wanted nothing bad to happen to you, but you wanted me to tame you…"

"Yes, that is true," said the fox.

"But now you are saying that you feel like crying," said the little prince.

"Indeed," said the fox.

"So, you have gained nothing!"

"I have gained the color of wheat,"

said the fox. Then, he added:

"Go and see the roses again. Now you will understand that your own flower is singular in the whole world. Then come back to say farewell to me, and I will tell you a secret as a farewell present."

The little prince went back to see the roses:

"You are not at all like my own rose; you are nothing yet," said the little prince to the roses. "Nobody has tamed you, and you have tamed no one, either. You are like what my fox once used to be. He was just a regular fox, like one hundred thousand other foxes. But I have made him my friend, and now he is unique in all the world."

And the roses grew very embarrassed.

"You are beautiful, but you are empty," said the little prince to the roses again. "Nobody would die for you. Of course, my own rose, an ordinary passer-by would think that she looks just like you. However, she is much more important than all of you combined, because it is her that I have watered. Because it is over her that I have placed a glass globe. Because it is her that I have sheltered behind a screen. Because it is for her that I have killed

the caterpillars, saving only two or three, so that they could change themselves into butterflies. Because it is her that I listened to, when she complained, or bragged, or even stopped talking. Because she is my rose."

And the little prince came back to the fox:

"Good bye," said little prince.

"Good bye," said the fox. "Here is my secret. It is very simple: It is only with the heart that we can see clearly. What is essential is invisible to the eye."

"What is essential is invisible to the eye," repeated the little prince, in order to remember it.

"It is the time that you have wasted for your rose that makes her so important."

"It is the time that I have wasted for my rose…" said the little prince, so that he could remember it.

"People easily forget this truth," said the fox. "But you must not forget it. You must be responsible forever for what you have tamed. You are responsible for your rose…"

"I am responsible for my rose," repeated the little prince, in order that he could remember it.

22

"Hello," said the little prince.

"Hello," replied the railroad switchman.

"What do you do here?" asked the little prince.

"I sort out travelers, in batches of a thousand," said the switchman. "I send trains that carry travelers, sometimes to the right, other times to the left."

Just then, a brightly lit express train shook the switchman's cabin, as it was rushing by like roaring thunder.

"They must be in a great hurry," said the little prince. "What are they looking for?"

"Not even the locomotive driver knows that," answered the switchman.

Coming in the opposite direction, a second brightly lit express train thundered by.

"Have they come back already?" asked the little prince.

"They are not the same ones," said the switchman. "This is an exchange."

"Are they not content with where they were?"

"No one is content with where he is," said the switchman.

Roaring like thunder, a third brightly lit express train rushed by.

"Are they chasing the first travelers?" asked the little prince.

"They are chasing nobody," said the switchman. "They are sleeping in there, or yawning a lot. Only the children are squashing their noses against the windowpanes."

"Only the children know what they are looking for," said the little prince. "They waste their time over a doll made of rags, and it is very important to them, and if you took the doll away from them, they would cry…"

"They are lucky," said the switchman.

23

"Good morning," said the little prince.

"Good morning," answered the merchant.

This was a merchant who was selling pills that perfectly quench thirst. If you swallowed one pill once per week, then you would feel no need to drink anything.

"Why do you sell those pills?" demanded the little prince.

"Because they save a lot of time," replied the merchant. "Experts have done the math. They say that you can save fifty-three minutes every week."

"What do you do with the fifty-three minutes?"

"I can do whatever I want to do."

The little prince said to himself:

'As for me, if I had the fifty-three minutes to spend, I would walk in a leisurely manner toward a fountain of water.'

24

It was now the eighth day since my airplane had broken down in the desert, and I had listened to the story of the merchant as I was drinking the last drop of my water supply.

I said to the little prince:

"Oh! Your memories, they are very pretty, but I have not repaired my airplane yet. I have nothing more to drink. So I would be happy, too, if I could walk in no haste toward a fountain of water."

"My friend, the fox, he told me…"

"My little friend, this is no longer a matter that pertains to the fox!"

"Why not?"

"Because we are going to die of thirst…"

He did not understand my words. He said to me:

"It is good to have had a friend, even if you are going to die. As for me, I am very content with having had a fox friend…"

I thought to myself:

'He does not realize the danger. He has not experienced hunger or thirst. Just a little bit of sunshine is enough for him.'

But the little prince looked at me and read my thoughts:

"I feel thirsty, too. Let's look for a well…"

I made a gesture of hopelessness. It is senseless to look for a well, aimlessly, in the vast desert. Nonetheless, we started to walk.

When we had trudged for several hours in silence, the night fell, and the stars began to light up. Being feverish with thirst, I saw them as if in a dream. The words of the little prince were dancing in my mind:

"So are you thirsty, too?" I asked him.

However, the little prince made no reply. He simply said to me:

"Water will be good for the heart, too…"

I did not understand his reply, but I remained in silence. I knew very well by then that it was useless to cross-examine him.

The little prince grew tired. He sat down. I sat down next to him. After falling silent, he said again:

"The stars are beautiful because of a flower that cannot be seen…"

"Indeed," I said, and in silence I gazed across the ridges of sand stretched out under the moon.

"The desert is beautiful," he added.

That was true. I have always loved the desert. You sit upon a dune of sand. You see nothing; you hear nothing. Nevertheless, something is radiant in the silence.

"What embellishes the desert," said the little prince, "is that somewhere out there it hides a well."

All of a sudden, I was surprised to comprehend the mysterious radiance of the sand. When I was a little boy, I lived in an old house, and according to legend, treasure had been buried there. Of course, nobody discovered it, and perhaps they had not even tried to look for it. But the legend of the treasure made the house enchanting. My house had a secret hidden at the bottom of its heart.

"Yes," I said to the little prince. "When it comes to a house, the stars, or the desert, what makes them beautiful is invisible!"

"I am content," said the little prince, "because you agree with my fox friend."

Because the little prince had fallen asleep, I carried him in my arms and started walking again. My heart was touched. I felt as if I were carrying a fragile treasure. It seemed to me that there was nothing more fragile on all of Earth. In the moonlight, I looked at his pale forehead, his closed eyes, the locks of his hair that waved in the wind, and I said to myself:

'What I see here is only the shell. What is most important is invisible…'

Because his slightly parted lips moved in a half-smile, I said to myself again:

'What touches me so deeply about this little prince who is

sleeping is his loyalty to a single flower, the image of that one rose that shines in him like the flame of a lamp, even when he is sleeping.'

And I felt that he was yet more fragile. You must protect lamps because one gust of wind can blow them out.

And having marched along in this way, I discovered a well at the break of day.

25

The little prince said:

"People, they rush about in express trains, but they no longer know what they are looking for. That is why they bustle about and 'go round and round'."

And he added:

"It is all in vain."

The well that we had arrived at was not like the Saharan wells. The Saharan wells are simple holes dug in the sand. This well was like the wells in towns. But there was no town there, and I thought I must have been dreaming.

"It is strange," I said to the little prince. "Everything is ready here: the pulley, the bucket, and the rope…"

The little prince laughed, touched the rope, and made the pulley start working. And the pulley squeaked like an old weathervane after the wind sleeps for a long while.

"Can you hear it?" said the little prince. "We have awakened the well, and it chants…"

I did not want him to strain himself:

"Leave it to me," I said to him. "It is too heavy for you."

Slowly, I pulled the bucket up to the rim of the well. Then, I set it there very carefully. The chanting of the pulley continued in my ears, and in the water that was still rippling I saw the sun rippling gently, too.

"I am thirsty for this water," said the little prince. "Give me some water to drink…"

And then I understood what he had been looking for!

I lifted the bucket up to his lips. He drank with his eyes closed. It was as sweet as a feast. The water was quite different from any ordinary nourishment. It was born out of the walk under the stars, of the chant of the pulley, and of the labor of my arms. It was good for the heart, like a present. When I was a little boy, the light of the Christmas tree, the music of the midnight Mass, and the softness of smiles all added up to the radiance of the Christmas presents that I received.

"People on your planet," said the little prince, "grow five thousand roses in a single garden, but they do not find in it what they are looking for…"

"They do not find what they are looking for," I agreed.

"And what you are looking for can be found in one single rose or in one sip of water."

"Indeed," I said.

And the little prince added:

"But the eyes are blind. You must look with your heart…"

I drank. It grew much easier to breathe. The sand at the break of day is the color of honey. I was also happy because of the color of honey. So why then did I feel sadness?

The little prince, who was sitting next to me once again, gently said to me:

"You must keep your promise."

"What promise?"

"You know…a muzzle for my sheep…I am responsible for the flower."

I pulled out my sketches from my pocket. The little prince looked at them, laughed, and said:

"Your baobab trees, they look a little bit like cabbages."

"Oh!" I had been so proud of my trees!

"Your fox…his ears…they look a bit like horns…and they are too long."

And he laughed again.

"You are unfair, my little friend. I know nothing about drawing, except the insides and the outsides of boa constrictors."

"Oh! That will do," he said. "Children will understand."

So, I did a sketch of a muzzle. And I felt my heart aching as I gave the drawing to him:

"You have plans that I do not know about…"

But he made no reply to me. He said to me instead:

"You know, my fall to the Earth…tomorrow will be the anniversary."

After some silence, the little prince continued:

"I fell very close to here."

And he flushed.

And again, without knowing why, I had a strange feeling of sadness. Nonetheless, one question occurred to me:

"So, it was not by chance that the morning when I met you eight days ago that you had been on a walk like that, all alone, a thousand miles away from where anyone lives. Were you on your way back to the place where you had fallen?"

The little prince flushed again.

And I added, hesitatingly:

"Perhaps it was because of the anniversary?"

The little prince flushed once again. He never answered my questions, but when he flushes, does not it mean "yes"?

"Oh!" I said to him. "I am frightened…"

Finally, he said to me:

"Now, you must work. You should go back to your airplane. I will be waiting for you here. Come back tomorrow evening…"

However, I was not reassured. I remembered the fox. You take the risk of crying a little if you allow yourself to be tamed.

26

Next to the well, there was the ruin of an old stone wall. When I came back from my work the following evening, I saw from a distance that my little prince was sitting there, with his legs dangling. And I heard him saying:

"So, you don't remember it, do you? It is certainly not here!"

Another voice must have answered him, because he replied:

"All right, all right, today is the right day, but this is not the right place."

I continued my walk toward the wall. I neither saw nor heard anyone else. Yet the little prince answered once again:

"Of course! You will see where my footprints start in the sand. All you have to do is to wait for me there. I shall be there tonight…"

I was twenty meters away from the wall, and still I saw nothing. The little prince said once again, after a silence:

"Do you have good venom? Are you sure that you will not make me suffer too long?"

I stopped, my heart feeling squeezed, but I still did not understand.

"Now, go away," said the little prince. "I would like to come down."

Then, I lowered my eyes toward the foot of the wall, and I leapt into the air! Raised up toward the little prince, there was one of the yellow snakes that can kill you in thirty seconds. Searching my pocket to draw my revolver, I took a running step, but at the sound I made, the snake softly slid into the sand, like a spouting of water dying out, and slipped among the stones with a light sound of metal, in no hurry.

I arrived at the wall just in time to catch my little prince in my arms. His face was as white as snow.

"What does this mean? Now you are talking with snakes?"

I loosened the golden scarf that he always wore. I dabbed his temples with water and made him drink. And I did not dare to ask him any more. He looked at me gravely, and wrapped his arms around my neck. I felt his heart beating, like the heart of a dying bird that has been shot with a rifle.

He said to me:

"I am glad because you have discovered the problem with your machine. Now you will be able to go back home."

"How did you know about that?"

I was just going to tell him that, against all expectations, my labor had been successful!

He never replied to my question, but he continued instead:

"I myself will go back home today, too."

And he added in a sad tone:

"It is much farther…it is much more difficult…"

I sensed clearly that something extraordinary was happening. In my arms, I was holding the little prince like a small child. However, it seemed to me that he was sinking directly into an abyss, with me being unable to hold him back from it.

He had a serious look, like someone lost somewhere far away.

"I have your drawing of the sheep. And I have the box for the sheep. And I have the muzzle."

And he smiled sadly.

I waited for a long time. I felt him reviving little by little:

"Little friend, you were frightened."

He was afraid, of course. However, he gently laughed:

"I shall be much more afraid this evening…"

Once again, I was chilled with the sense of something irreparable. And I knew that I could not bear the idea of no longer hearing that laughter. For me, it was like a spring of water in the desert.

"Little friend, I would like to hear you laugh once more."

But he said to me:

"Tonight, it will be one year. My planet will find itself right above the place where I fell last year."

"Little friend, isn't it just a bad dream, the talking with the snake, and the rendezvous, and the star?"

However, the little prince made no answer. He said to me instead:

"What is important, you cannot see."

"Of course."

"It is as it was with the flower. If you love a flower that lives on a star, it is sweet at night to look at the sky. All the stars are blooming with flowers."

"Yes, of course."

"It is as it was with the water, too. What you gave me to drink was like music, because of the pulley, and the rope. You remember…how sweet it was."

"Yes, indeed."

"You will see the stars at night. My planet is so small that I cannot show you where you can find it. It is better like that. My star will be but one of many stars to you. Then, all of the stars, you will love to look at them. They will all be your friends. And I will give you a present."

He laughed once again.

"Oh! Little friend, my little friend, I love to hear that laughter!"

"That will be just my present. It will be as it was with the water."

"What do you mean?"

"To people the stars are not all the same. For those who travel, the stars are guides. For others, they are no more than little lights. For others, who are scholars, they are problems to solve. For the businessman I met, they were gold. However, all of those stars are silent. As for you, you will have the stars that no one else has."

"What do you mean?"

"When you look at the sky at night, because I live on one of the stars, because I shall laugh on one of them, it will be as if all the stars were laughing. You will have stars that can laugh!"

And he laughed once more.

"And when you are consoled (people always find consolation in the end), you will be happy because you have known me. You will be my friend forever. You will wish you could laugh with me. And often you will open your window, like so, for pleasure. And your friends will be surprised to see you laugh as you are looking across the sky. Then you will tell them: 'Yes, the stars, they always make me laugh!' And they will think you are crazy. And that will be a wicked trick that I will have played on you…"

And he laughed again.

"It will be as if I had given you, in place of the stars, piles of small bells that can laugh."

And he laughed again. Then he became serious once more:

"Tonight…you know…don't come to me."

"I will not leave you."

"I shall look as if I were sick. I shall look a bit like I was dying. It's like that. Do not come to see it. It is not worth it."

"I will not leave you."

But he grew worried.

"I am telling you this…it is also because of the snake. It must not bite you. Snakes, they are vicious. They might bite just for fun."

"I will not leave you."

However, something reassured him:

"It is true that snakes have no more venom for a second bite."

That night, I did not see him set off. He slipped away without a sound. When I finally caught up with him, he walked with determination, at a fast pace. He only said to me:

"Oh! You are here…"

And he took me by the hand. But he grew worried again.

"You made the wrong decision. You will suffer. I shall look as if I was dying, but it will be not real…"

I fell silent.

"You understand. It is too far. I cannot take this body along with me. It is too heavy."

I said nothing.

"But it will be like old, abandoned bark. It is not sad, old bark."

I stayed silent.

He became a bit discouraged. But he made an effort once again:

"It will be gentle, you know. I myself will look at the stars. All of the stars will be like wells with rusty pulleys. All of the stars will pour me something to drink…"

I kept my silence.

"It will be such fun! You will have five hundred million little bells, and I will have five hundred million fountains of water."

And then he too fell silent because he was crying.

"Here we are. Let me go on all alone from here."

And he sat down because he was fearful. Then he said again:

"You know…my flower, I am responsible for her! And she is so weak. And she is so naive. She only has four thorns that are of no use at all to protect her against the world."

As for me, I sat down too because I could no longer stand.

He said:

"You see…that is all…"

He hesitated again a bit, and then he got up. He took one step. I myself could not move. There was nothing else but something yellow flashing around his ankle. He stood still for a moment. He did not cry. Then, he fell gently, as a tree falls. His fall made no sound because of the sand.

27

And now, indeed, it has already been six years. I have never spoken of this story before. My friends, upon seeing me again, were very happy to see me back alive. I was sad, but I told them:

"I am just tired."

Now I am consoled a little. Of course, not completely, I mean. But I know for certain that the little prince went back to his planet because, at the break of day, I could not find his body. It was not so heavy a body after all. And I love to listen to the stars at night. They are like five hundred million little bells.

However, there is something extraordinary. The muzzle that

I drew for the little prince, I forgot to add a leather strap to it. He will never be able to fasten it onto the sheep.

So I keep wondering:

'What has been happening on his planet? Perhaps the sheep has eaten the flower…'

Sometimes, I say to myself:

'Certainly not! The little prince secures his flower under the glass globe every night, and he watches over his sheep very closely.'

Then, I feel happy. And all of the stars laugh sweetly.

At other times, I think to myself:

'People can be distracted at times, and that is enough! The little prince perhaps forgot, one evening, the glass globe, or the sheep escaped, making no noise, at night…'

Then, all the little bells turn into tears.

This is the real, great mystery. For you who also love the little prince, as for me, nothing in the universe can be the same if somewhere a sheep, that we do not know, has eaten (or not eaten) a rose, though we do not know exactly where.

Look up at the sky. Then, ask yourself:

'Did, or did not, the sheep eat the flower?'

And you will see how everything changes…

And no grown-up will ever understand that it is of great importance.

For me, this is the most beautiful and the saddest landscape in the world. It is the same landscape shown on the previous page, but I drew it once more in order to show it to you better. It is in this scene on Earth that the little prince appeared and departed.

Look at the landscape attentively so that you may recognize it if you travel some day in Africa, in the desert. And if you happen to pass through there, I beg you, do not hurry, but pause a little right under the star. Then, if a child comes to you, if he laughs, if he has golden hair, and if he makes no reply to your questions, then you can guess who he is. Then, please be so kind! Don't leave me in great sorrow, but instead write to me quickly that he has come back...

The Little Prince

Author: Antoine de Saint-Exupéry | **Translator:** Juok Yoon | **Illustrator:** Minji Kim

Publisher: Jonggil Kim | **Publishing Co.:** Indigo

Publication Register: No.7-312

Address: 395-151 Daeryung Bldg. 4F, Seogyo-dong, Mapo-gu, Seoul, Korea. **Postal Code:** 121-840

Tel: 02-998-7030 **Fax:** 02-998-7924 **Email:** geuldam4u@geuldam.com | **Website:** indigostory.co.kr

Blog: http://blog.naver.com/geuldam4u | **Facebook:** www.facebook.com/geuldam4u

First Printing: April 25, 2015 **First Print Eighth Run Release:** May 20, 2024

ISBN 978-89-92632-91-1 03860

이 도서의 국립중앙도서관 출판시도서목록(CIP)은 e-CIP홈페이지(http://www.nl.go.kr/ecip)와
국가자료공동목록시스템(http://www.nl.go.kr/kolisnet)에서 이용하실 수 있습니다. (CIP 제어번호 : CIP2015010412)